Made in United States
Orlando, FL
19 May 2023

33291900R00067